I Lost My Sock

By Lin Jakary

Illustrated by Ryan Olson

WOCTO PUBLISHING • LA JOLLA

ISBN: 978-1-934867-01-3
Library of Congress Control Number: 2008920586

Printed in the United States of America

First Edition

www.wocto.com

This book belongs to:

_____

Did the dryer eat it?
I don't know.

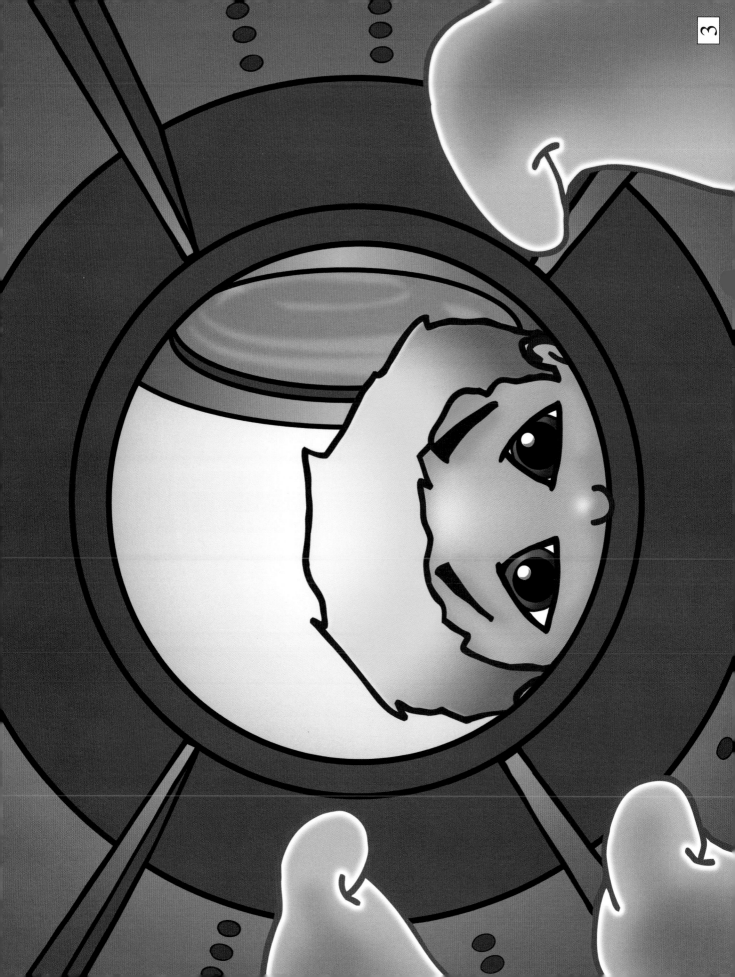

Maybe it jumped off the sink.
Wheeeee!

9

Did it jump because
my feet are stinky?

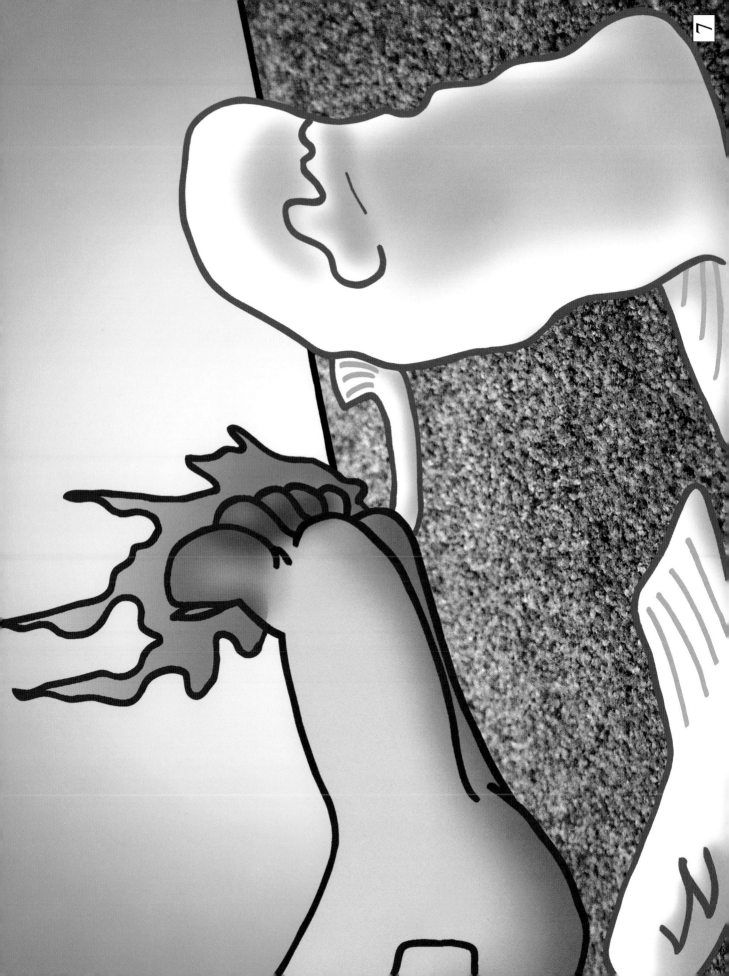

7

Did doggy give it
quite a fright?

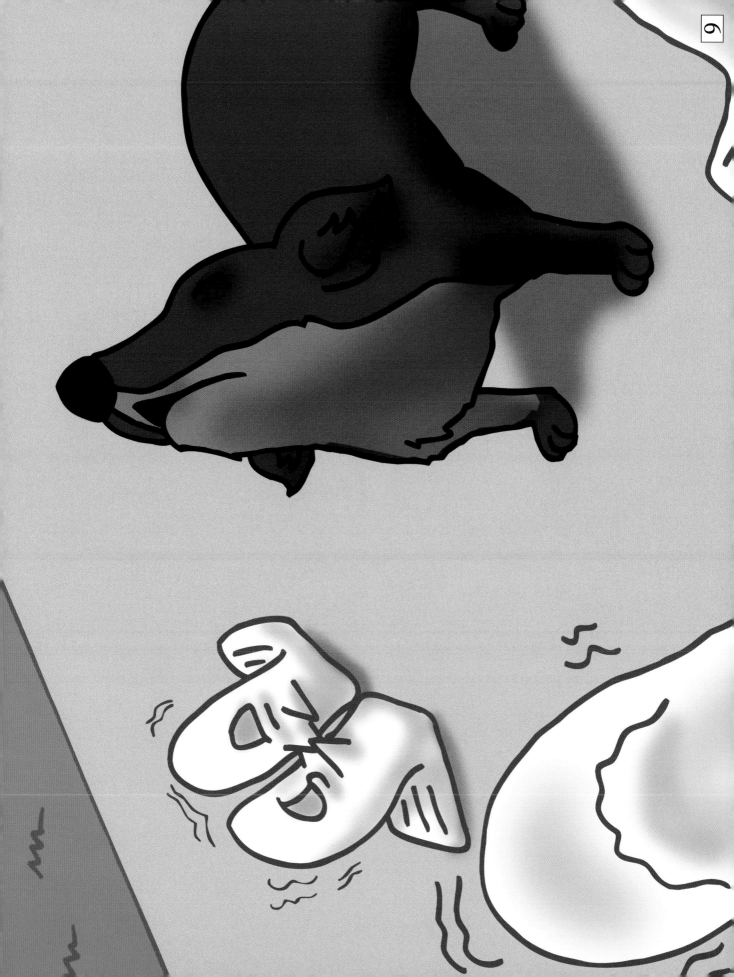

Did it slip out the back door late at night?

One by one
or two by two
was it unhappy
in my shoe?

Where is my sock?
Will it stay stray
or pair up at a party
in the Cays?

Did it wander off
to other feet,

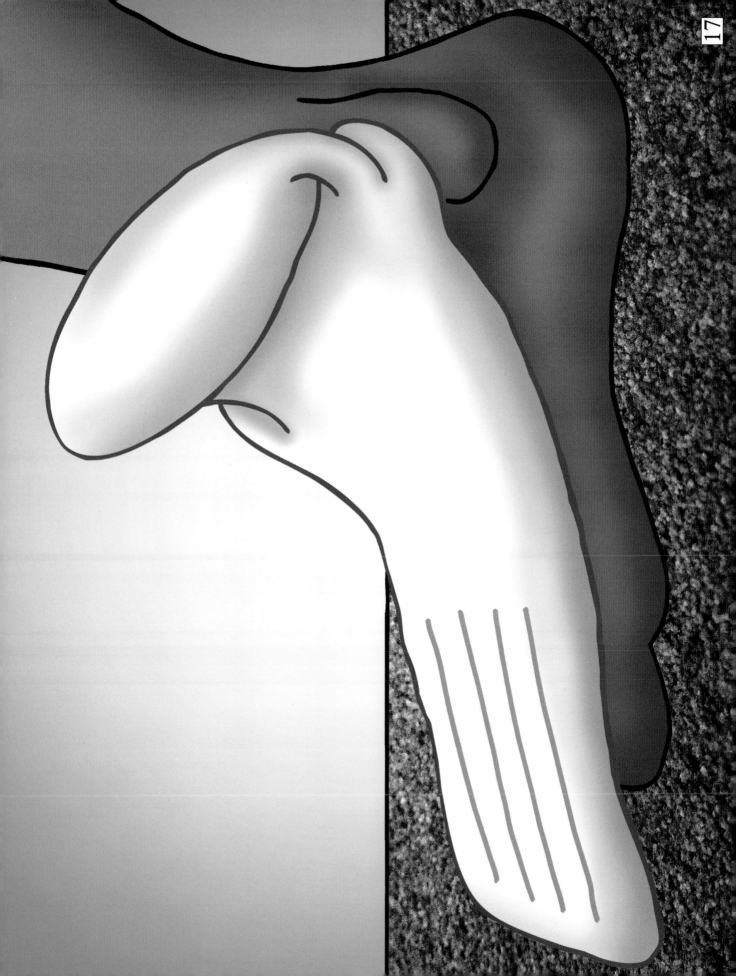

and end up in a drawer
so neat?

Should I put up signs
on city blocks?
Missing, have you seen this sock?

Will people think
I am a bore
because my socks
have run away before?

23

24

Is the white one in
an all-night diner?

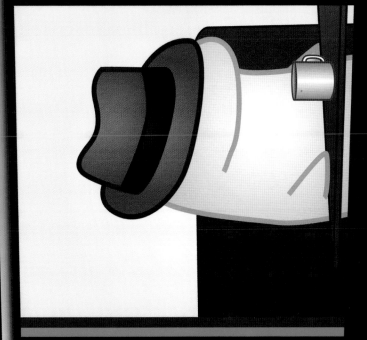

Is the brown one on
a boat to China?

Is the striped one on a flight
to Rome?

Is the blue one trying to
come home?

Sock Alert!

My sock is history, and will remain another mystery.

Has your sock ever disappeared?